Custer

The Last Cavalier

Paal Loncle

Published by Books Sphere LLC
www.bookssphere.com
Grand Junction, CO.

ISBN: 978-1-968766-13-9

First Edition: 2026

Printed in the United States of America

Reveille

The morning light crept slowly over the Union camp, painting the canvas tents and stacked rifles in a pale gold haze. Bugles broke the silence, calling out the *Reveille* in a chorus that carried across the dew-damp fields. Horses stamped in their enclosures, and men stirred from their blankets, rubbing sleep from their eyes as the sun began its climb.

Amid the sound of horns and murmured prayers, General George Armstrong Custer sat motionless upon his horse. The blue of his uniform was sharp against the dawn. A dark, commanding silhouette beneath the fluttering folds of the 1863 Union flag. Gold braids glimmered along his collar; two bright stars winked from his epaulettes. His ivory gloves gripped the reins lightly, while the curls of his golden hair spilled from beneath his cavalry hat like threads of sunlight.

He was young for a general, but no one could deny the aura that surrounded him, the kind of confidence that burned dangerously close to vanity. When the final notes of the bugle faded, Custer dismounted in one smooth motion, his boots striking the earth with purpose. Around him, rows of soldiers straightened to attention.

Custer stood before them, surveying their faces, men hardened by campaign, yet still young enough to believe in glory. He drew in a long breath and began to speak, his voice cutting through the stillness like a saber's edge.

"I want all you men to remember," he declared, "that a true American soldier destroys his enemy by making him perish on the battlefield. Any man who loves his country relishes the fight, and he will gladly give his life to see his nation's enemies destroyed."

The men listened in solemn silence. A breeze lifted the flag above him, its stripes snapping softly.

"All real soldiers," he went on, "love the smell of blood and death on the battlefield. As it was for Joshua at Jericho, for King David at Canaan, for Alexander in Persia, and for Robert the Bruce at Bannockburn; defeat is shameful, and it cannot, it *must not*, be tolerated."

He paused, scanning their faces; young, grim, inspired.

"We must advance on the enemy at all costs," he said. "For my part, I am happy. Happy to lead you men against any foe, and at any price, be it life or limb. That is all."

The air held his words long after he had finished. For a moment, the camp seemed to stand outside of time, the soldiers staring at the man who had spoken as if he were both prophet and warrior. Then a murmur rose among them, low but steady, a current of resolve.

Custer turned back to his horse and mounted with the ease of habit. As he saluted toward the rising sun, the bugles sounded again, this time not as a summons to wake, but as a call to destiny.

He believed, with every beat of his fervent heart, that God had made him for war.

1862

Lessons from Antietam

The smell of death clung to the Maryland air like damp smoke. The battle at Antietam had ended, but the ground still trembled with memory, the echo of cannon fire, the screams of the dying. The fields were soaked through with blood, and the corpses of men and horses lay tangled together among shattered wagons and splintered wheels. Flies swarmed over the ruin.

Vultures circled lazily in the gray sky, descending now and again to tear at flesh. Nearby villagers picked through the wreckage, scavenging trinkets and rifles, cutting buttons from blue and gray jackets alike. The Civil War had not yet taught them shame.

The looting ended abruptly when a column of Union officers appeared on horseback, their silhouettes emerging through the smoke like avenging spirits. The villagers scattered, vanishing into the distant tree line.

One officer, his voice harsh and exhausted, surveyed the devastation and muttered, "Goddammit, what a bloody mess."

Beside him rode Major General George Meade, his face pale and grim. "Looks like the papers got it right," he said quietly.

The first officer consulted a crumpled list. "Forty supply wagons destroyed. Sixteen cannons gone. Fifty-six horses. Two hundred pounds of ammunition lost. Sixteen hundred wounded, a hundred missing, six hundred dead." He lowered the paper. "These are the totals for the division."

Meade drew a long breath, his eyes scanning the field of ruin. "God Almighty," he said, almost to himself. "We need a cavalry officer who can strike the enemy where it hurts and spare our men this slaughter."

The officer turned in his saddle. "You wouldn't be thinking of that West Point troublemaker, would you? That Custer boy?"

Meade's eyes narrowed, the corners of his mouth tightening in a faint smile. "Quite possibly so."

The other man groaned and crossed himself. "Lord have mercy."

They rode on in silence for a while, their horses stepping carefully among the dead.

Far off, the wind carried the faint, mournful sound of a bugle, its notes bending and breaking over the valley like a prayer for the fallen.

And somewhere beyond the haze of smoke and carrion, George Armstrong Custer was waiting for his

chance, young, ambitious, and still untested by the horrors
that would soon make his name both celebrated and cursed.

The war had given him his stage. He only needed the
curtain to rise.

1863

Promotion to General

By the summer of 1863, the air in Washington was thick with rumors and the restless pulse of a nation at war. Armies shifted like tides across the East, and every victory or defeat seemed to alter the very balance of the Union. Among the officers stationed near the capital, one name began to surface more often George Armstrong Custer, the impetuous young cavalryman whose ambition was as sharp as his saber.

On the morning of June 29, the rail yard at Washington buzzed with energy. A brass band stood ready on the platform, their instruments gleaming in the heat of the rising sun. Flags rippled from the rooftops, and soldiers; dusty, sunburned, and half-starved from campaign life, gathered to witness a ceremony that promised a taste of glory.

Custer stood upon the balcony of a waiting train car, his uniform a crisp blue trimmed with gold. The curls of his hair glowed like burnished metal beneath his cap. His boots, polished to mirror brightness, reflected the sunlight as though even the heavens acknowledged him. He was about to receive his commission as acting Major General of the Michigan Cavalry Brigade, soon to be known across the battlefields as *Custer's Wolverines*.

Before him stood General Alfred Pleasonton, stern and formal, holding the official document in his gloved hand. The murmur of the assembled crowd faded as Pleasonton cleared his throat.

"Let the record reflect," he announced, "that on this day, June 29, in the year of our Lord eighteen hundred and sixty-three, George Armstrong Custer is hereby promoted to acting Major General."

The band struck up a triumphant chord as applause thundered across the platform. Custer stepped forward, bowed slightly, and said, "Thank you, sir."

"Congratulations, George," Pleasonton replied, clasping his hand.

From somewhere in the crowd a soldier shouted, "All hail the Wolverines!" and a cheer rolled through the ranks, "Hurrah! Hurrah!" The band responded with *The Battle Cry of Freedom,* its notes piercing the humid air as the newly promoted general looked down upon his men.

Pleasonton turned to him with a half-smile. "What do you think of this magnificent parade, George?"

Custer's lips curved into a grin. "Well, sir," he said, "I can't tell if I'm in one of Shakespeare's great plays or marching off to battle with King David."

Pleasonton laughed, but beneath his amusement lingered something more complicated, a flicker of concern, perhaps, or envy. He knew ambition when he saw it, and in Custer it burned like a fever.

The music swelled as the Michigan Brigade began its march, banners flying and sabers glinting in the sun. The crowd roared again, and Custer, ever the showman, raised his hat in salute. The cheers followed him long after the train had rolled away, echoing in his mind like a promise of destiny fulfilled.

July 1863

Gettysburg

Morning broke over Pennsylvania like the slow opening of a wound. The hills near Gettysburg were wrapped in mist, and from the haze came the dull concussion of artillery; steady, deliberate, the sound of war at its full awakening.

General George Armstrong Custer emerged from his tent, Bible in hand, the gilt letters of his name catching the pale dawn light. A young orderly rushed forward, breathless, eyes wide.
"Sir! the Rebs are attacking Gettysburg. General Lee himself leads them."

Custer's expression did not change. He slid the Bible shut, fastened his sword belt, and said quietly, "Then it is God's will we meet them there. Fetch my horse."

By midmorning, the Michigan Cavalry Brigade stood in formation atop a ridge overlooking the valley. Cannon smoke rolled toward them like storm clouds. Custer, barely twenty-three, sat his horse with the poise of a man twice his age; golden hair catching the wind, eyes alight with the thrill of combat.

A courier galloped up the slope. "General Meade orders you to take that road and hold it at all costs!"

Custer grinned, the reckless, holy grin of a man who saw destiny ahead. "At all costs," he repeated, then turned to his men. "Come on, you Wolverines!"

They roared back, a single voice of defiance, and charged. The world became thunder and flame. Horses plunged into the smoke, sabers flashed like lightning, and men screamed as blue met gray in the choking fields below. The battle raged for hours and by the third day, the Confederate advance was broken.

That night, as silence settled over the corpses and smoldering guns, Custer stood alone among his men. The moonlight caught the edge of his sword.

"As Moses parted the Red Sea," he murmured, "so have we parted death from victory. Do not mourn the fallen, their blood was not spilled in vain."

The men lifted their hats in weary salute. Somewhere beyond the ridge, a bugler began to play *The Battle Hymn of the Republic*. Its notes drifted across the dark fields, mingling with the ghosts of the day.

1863

Stagnant Service

The smoke of Gettysburg had barely cleared when glory began to sour. The campfires burned low at night, and laughter, once easy, triumphant, had turned to grumbling. The Michigan Cavalry Brigade, bled white by the summer's battles, found itself idle in the humid lull of late 1863. Idleness, for soldiers accustomed to war, was its own kind of poison.

In the stillness of camp, discipline frayed. Cards replaced drills; whiskey replaced prayers. Men wandered from their tents into nearby towns, returning with stolen trinkets, stories, and guilt. A few never returned at all. Custer rode the lines each morning, the heel of his boot tapping the horse's flank in agitation, his temper coiled and restless. Glory was a fire that needed feeding, and he had no battle left to feed it.

It was during one of these mornings that a sergeant came to him, hat in hand. "Sir," the man began, hesitating, "we've got a deserter. Private in Second Company. Says he's suffering from battle fatigue."

Custer turned sharply, his blue eyes hardening. "Battle fatigue? There's nothing wrong with that man except cowardice." He dismounted in one quick motion. "Tie him to a post and flog him in front of the regiment. Let every man here see what happens to those who run from duty."

The sergeant swallowed. "Yes, sir."

By midday, the soldiers had gathered in a semicircle before the punishment post. The condemned private, young, trembling, barely more than a boy, stood bound, tears streaking the dirt on his face. Custer rode before his men, his voice steady and cold.

"This man," he declared, "abandoned his post to save his own skin while the rest of you stayed to fight. He is no soldier of the Union, but a disgrace to it. Sergeant, proceed."

The whip cracked once, then again. The boy screamed, and Custer did not flinch. The men shifted uneasily, some looking away, others staring in silence as the lashes fell. When it was over, the private was cut loose and carried to the field hospital. The sound of his sobs lingered long after the men dispersed.

A week later, newspapers carried whispers of the flogging. Correspondents had been in camp that day, unseen but listening. The report reached General Meade, and before long, Custer was summoned to headquarters in Maryland.

The general's tent smelled of pipe smoke and damp canvas. "George," Meade began, his expression unreadable, "I believe you know why you're here."

Custer nodded stiffly. "Yes, sir."

Meade's voice hardened. "It grieves me to see such inhuman treatment of men under your command. You flogged that soldier like a slave, and the War Department won't overlook it."

"I meant no harm, sir," Custer said quickly. "The man deserted. I sought to preserve order."

"Order?" Meade's eyes narrowed. "Do you realize how our enemies treat their negro slaves, flogging, beating, degrading them? You've done the same to your own man. The Chief of Staff will decide your fate, not I. You'd best pray he finds mercy."

Custer's jaw tightened. "I only ever wished to serve, sir, to lead men in battle. That is where I belong."

"It may no longer be your choice," Meade replied quietly. "You're dismissed."

That night, back in camp, Custer sat in silence, staring into the fire. His aide-de-camp offered him coffee; he refused it. The men avoided his tent, afraid of his silence. When at last he spoke, his voice carried the strain of a man wrestling both pride and faith.

"I was made for battle," he said. "God sent me to be a warrior, not to sit in disgrace. Why must I be punished for doing what was right?" His voice cracked slightly. "I would rather die in war than rot in shame."

Later, alone in the dim chapel tent, he knelt and pressed his hands together, whispering a prayer into the darkness.

"God, grant me the strength to endure these trials. I am flawed, I know — but do not forsake me. Even though I walk through the valley of the shadow of death, I will fear no evil. For Thou art with me."

When he rose, his eyes were dry. The fire outside had gone cold, but the one within him burned hotter than ever.

1864

The Shenandoah and the Wilderness

The early summer of 1864 dawned calm and green across Maryland, a deceptive peace that masked the grinding brutality of the war. For George Armstrong Custer, the weeks that followed his disgrace were marked by waiting, a condition he endured poorly. Every quiet morning felt like a judgment, every idle hour a threat to the destiny he believed God had carved for him.

When orders finally came, they arrived without ceremony. Custer was summoned east, his brigade ordered to accompany him. The message carried no praise, but neither did it carry condemnation. It was enough. He took it as a sign of mercy.

At headquarters, General Alfred Pleasonton greeted him with a measured smile. "George," he said, "how are you holding up?"

"Quite well, sir," Custer replied, though his voice betrayed the effort behind the words.

Pleasonton studied him for a moment. "The War Department has seen fit to give you division command. There's rebel movement in the Shenandoah Valley, we're not yet sure of its purpose."

Custer's eyes lit with restrained relief. "Yes sir. I've heard rumors."

"Make no mistake," Pleasonton continued, lowering his voice. "You're on a short leash. Had it been my decision, I might have relieved you entirely."

"I understand," Custer said. "Only give me the chance to fight. The South is weakening. I will not let this war end without doing my part."

Pleasonton nodded slowly. "Your division will remain on alert. If the rebels move, you'll be sent straight into their flank."

"Thank you, sir," Custer replied. "I won't fail you — so long as God stands witness."

Two weeks later, the Confederacy made its move.

General Robert E. Lee, desperate and increasingly ill-supplied, drove his forces through the Shenandoah Valley in a final gamble. If Washington could be threatened, perhaps the Union's resolve might fracture. It was a bold, reckless plan and one the Union could not allow to succeed.

At army headquarters, Meade gathered his commanders. Maps lay spread across the table, marked with red and blue ink.

"The rebels have struck in the southern valley," Meade said grimly. "Our men are surrounded in the Wilderness. I need a commander willing to move fast, to carve a path through their flank and restore our supply lines."

Silence followed.

Then Custer stepped forward. "Sir, I can strike their southern road within three days. Two battalions will be enough. Cut off their supplies and relieve our men."

Meade looked at him long and hard. "What you ask is nearly impossible. The casualties will be severe."

"I have full confidence in my men," Custer replied. "The enemy is desperate. They will fight hard, but they are hungry, ill-supplied, and nearing the end."

Orders were given. The Wolverines rode south.

The valley swallowed them whole, thick woods, narrow roads, and hidden ridges that turned every advance into a trap. Confederate regiments poured through the wilderness in gray waves, striking with ferocity born of despair. The Union cavalry was pushed hard, boxed against the high roads, and strained to the edge of exhaustion.

Supplies ran dangerously low. Horses collapsed in their traces. Men rationed water by mouthfuls.

In desperation, Custer summoned the unit chaplain.

"I need a prayer," he said. "One for food, water, and strength, and quickly."

By nightfall, the prayer was distributed across the division. Custer read it aloud by lantern light, his voice steady despite the fear tightening his chest.

"God of this Union," he prayed, "grant us the means to defeat those who would destroy this nation founded by free men. Give us food, water, and resolve. Let us not surrender to despair but stand firm in perseverance."

Three days later, supply wagons broke through the lines.

The men cheered, laughing and weeping in equal measure. With renewed strength, Custer drove the Confederates back toward their own positions, forcing retreat inch by bloody inch.

When the fighting finally paused, Custer raised a cup in salute. "To victory," he said, "and to the nearing end of this terrible war."

Cheers answered him, weary, hollow, but alive.

In a field hospital that evening, Custer paused beside a wounded Black soldier, his legs shattered.

"What happened to you, son?" Custer asked gently.

"Hit in both legs, sir."

Custer nodded. "You'll heal. I've seen worse." He smiled faintly. "You get well soon."

As he stepped back into the dusk, Custer felt the old fire return, the belief that redemption was still possible, that glory had not yet abandoned him.

The war, it seemed, was not finished with George Armstrong Custer.

1865

The Siege of Petersburg

By the winter of 1865, the war had become a thing of attrition, a slow, grinding exhaustion of men and will. Outside Petersburg, Virginia, the Union lines stretched like an iron noose around the last great artery feeding the Confederate capital. Trenches scarred the earth. The air was heavy with damp soil, smoke, and death that never fully cleared.

For George Armstrong Custer, the siege was a bitter vigil. The glory of sweeping charges had given way to waiting — waiting for orders, for surrender, for the war itself to die. He rode the lines daily, his men silent and gaunt, their blue coats faded by rain and blood. Victory was close now, close enough to taste, yet somehow joyless.

One cold morning, an orderly approached him. "Sir, General Grant requests your presence immediately."

Custer nodded and mounted without a word. Cannons boomed in the distance as he rode toward headquarters, the sound echoing like a funeral drum. He felt a strange mix of anticipation and unease. Ulysses S. Grant was not a man who summoned officers lightly.

Grant's headquarters were plain, almost austere. The general himself stood bent over a map, his uniform wrinkled and unadorned, his boots worn but clean. He looked up as Custer entered.

"George," Grant said, extending a hand. "I've been expecting you."

"Yes, sir," Custer replied.

Grant gestured to the map. "Lee is moving toward Amelia Court House. If we cut off his retreat and deprive him of supplies, we can force an end to this war. I want you to strike fast and block his escape."

Custer's eyes gleamed. "My men will give them the reckoning they deserve, sir."

Grant studied him carefully. "Do not mistake this for a hunt for glory. What you do now will shape what comes after, for you, and for the country."

"I understand," Custer said, though his heart thundered with anticipation.

The final clash came at Sayler's Creek. Cannon fire shattered the quiet countryside. Men charged through smoke and fire, shouting themselves hoarse. Custer rode at the head of his column, saber raised, his voice cutting through the chaos.

"Charge! Let no man escape! God help you!"

The Confederate line collapsed under the weight of Union force. Thousands surrendered. Others fled into the woods, their war finally broken.

When the guns fell silent, Custer stood amid the wreckage, breathing hard, his uniform smeared with mud and blood. It was over, though not yet officially.

1865

Appomattox

The small meeting house at Appomattox Court House stood quiet beneath a pale spring sky. Inside, the air was thick with tension and history.

General Robert E. Lee entered first, immaculate in gray, his uniform pressed and adorned with gold. His beard was neatly trimmed, his posture dignified despite defeat. Moments later, General Grant entered, dressed plainly in a private's uniform, his bearing humble and resolute.

Custer stood near the back of the room, surrounded by officers of higher rank. He watched in silence, his expression unreadable.

"This surrender will be unconditional," Grant said calmly. "Please sign here."

Lee nodded once. "Yes, sir."

The pens scratched softly across the paper. The war ended not with thunder, but with ink.

Lee rose. "Good day, gentlemen."

"Good day, General," Grant replied. "May God grant grace to you and your men."

When Lee departed, the room exhaled. Some officers smiled. Others wept. Grant turned and caught sight of Custer.

"You've done well, George," he said. "You've earned a rest. Report back to headquarters in three weeks."

Custer bowed his head. "Thank you, sir."

Outside, as he mounted his horse, the familiar strains of *The Battle Hymn of the Republic* drifted across the fields. Custer rode on alone, the cheers fading behind him.

The war that had made him was over.

1867

Fighting the Indians

Two years after the guns fell silent in Virginia, George Armstrong Custer found himself far from the cheering crowds and battle hymns of the East. The plains stretched endlessly before him, harsh, unforgiving, and indifferent to reputation. Here, glory was no longer granted by flags or bugles, but contested inch by inch against hunger, exhaustion, and an enemy who knew the land far better than he ever could.

Assigned to the western frontier, Custer led the 7th Cavalry against the Cheyenne, whose resistance grew fiercer with every broken treaty and stolen mile. Supplies were scarce. Rations were thin. Horses weakened under the relentless sun. The men grew restless, then resentful.

Still, Custer clung to resolve. "Hold fast," he told them. "The Jamestown settlers endured starvation and constant threat, and so shall we. Supplies will come."

But the frontier offered no guarantees.

One evening, his aide approached in haste. "Sir, our scouts report a large Cheyenne force gathering two miles from the garrison."

Custer's jaw tightened. "Men," he called out, "arm yourselves at once."

The attack came swiftly, a blur of gunfire, screams, and dust. Neither side claimed victory. Bodies lay scattered across the plain, Union blue mingled with buckskin and blood. For Custer, the battle was a defeat not only of arms, but of ambition. The war here did not reward boldness. It punished it.

1867

Run-ins with Subordinates

Supplies eventually arrived, but order did not return with them. The men drank heavily. Fights broke out nightly. Discipline, once rigid, crumbled beneath frontier fatigue.

Custer's patience snapped.

"We will have order in this brigade," he thundered, "or I will see every offender hanged or shot!"

Officers carried out his commands, imprisoning men, restoring order by fear where respect had faded. Journalists soon followed, drawn by rumors of tyranny.

"Sir," one asked, "is it true you're imprisoning men without cause?"

"No," Custer replied flatly. "And no law is being violated."

Another pressed him. "Is it true you said you'd scalp this whole unit if they disgraced you?"

Custer smiled thinly. "No. But I wish I had."

Laughter followed, but it was uneasy, edged with disbelief.

The frontier was watching now.

1867

Demotion and Court Martial

The reckoning came swiftly.

Custer stood before a military tribunal, his once-polished reputation worn thin. The charges were read, the verdict already inevitable.

"I sentence you," the judge said, "to one year's suspension and demotion to the rank of major. You are hereby stripped of command."

Custer stood rigid. When asked for final words, he spoke without bitterness.

"The greatest thing I ever did," he said, "was lead men in battle during the great Civil War. I thank those who stood beside me."

The gavel fell. His career, as he had known it, ended.

The next day, Alfred Pleasonton found him preparing for a ride.

"You were the best commander the war produced," Pleasonton said quietly. "That flogging incident back in '63, I believe it helped win the whole fight."

Custer nodded once. "Thank you, sir."

He rode out alone.

Final Monologue

There was a time, two thousand years ago, when our Lord rode upon a mule through crowds waving palm leaves and shouting praise. Days later, those same voices cried for His death.

Let this be our warning: that exaltation is fleeting, and glory fades as swiftly as it comes. What men raise up, they will one day cast down.

I have ridden at the head of armies and stood in the shadow of kings. I have known praise, and I have known disgrace. And in the end, all of it passes.

Only the judgment of history remains.